Megan's Balancing Act
by Susan Korman

Illustrations by
Bill Dodge

Spot Illustrations by
Rich Grote

MAGIC ATTIC PRESS

Published by Magic Attic Press.

Copyright ©1996 by MAGIC ATTIC PRESS

For more information contact:
Book Editor, Magic Attic Press, 866 Spring Street,
P.O. Box 9722, Portland, ME 04104-5022

First Edition
Printed in the United States of America
2 3 4 5 6 7 8 9 10

Magic Attic Club is a registered trademark.

Betsy Gould, Publisher
Marva Martin, Art Director
Robin Haywood, Managing Editor

Edited by Judit Bodnar
Designed by Cindy Vacek

With special thanks to Coach Debbie Rogers and the Bucks County
Country Day School Cougars, and Luan Peszek from USA Gymnastics.

ISBN 1-57513-092-0

Magic Attic Club books are printed on acid-free, recycled paper.

As members of the
MAGIC ATTIC CLUB,
we promise to
be best friends,
share all of our adventures in the attic,
use our imaginations,
have lots of fun together,
and remember—the real magic is in us.

Alison   Keisha

Heather   Megan

Contents

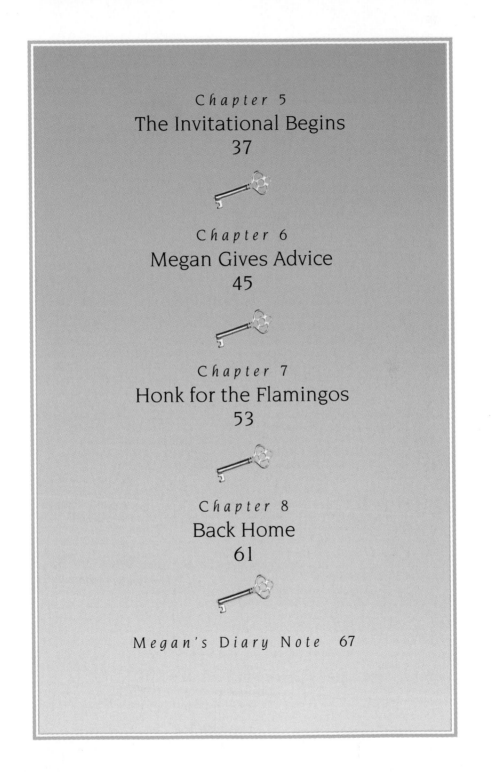

MEGAN
SITS IT OUT

ey, Alison! Megan!"

Megan Ryder and her three best friends, Alison McCann, Keisha Vance, and Heather Hardin, were riding their bikes along the path in the park. As they pedaled past the softball field, Megan heard someone call out their names.

"Stop, you guys!"

Megan saw a tall, dark-haired boy racing toward them, frantically waving to get their attention.

"Oh no." Alison groaned. "It's my brother Mark. I wonder what *he* wants."

"What's up, Mark? " Alison asked.

"A bunch of us are supposed to be playing softball," he answered, panting. He motioned toward the field, where a few kids were standing near the pitcher's mound. "But some of the players didn't show up, and I was wondering—"

"If we'd be on your team?" Alison jumped in.

Mark nodded. "The Wildcats are really good," he went on. "If we don't get at least two more players, they'll slaughter us."

Alison looked at her friends.

Megan could tell she was dying to play. "Do you guys feel like it?" she asked hopefully.

"Sure, I'll play," Keisha said.

"Me, too," Heather said. "If you guys want to."

Alison turned to Megan. "How about you, Megan?"

"Uh . . ." Megan flushed as she felt four pairs of eyes on her. "No, thanks," she said quickly. "You guys go ahead. I'll just watch."

"Are you sure?" Keisha asked. "We don't want to leave

you out."

"Honest, I don't mind," Megan reassured her friends. "I'm terrible at softball, remember? The last time we played with Mark's team, I struck out every single time."

"So what?" Alison said. "Come on. It'll be more fun if we all play."

"No thanks, Ali," Megan said, shaking her head. "I'd really rather just watch."

Mark started toward the field as the other team arrived carrying bats and gloves.

The girls quickly locked up their bikes and followed him. Alison, Keisha and Heather borrowed gloves and began to warm up. Megan dropped onto the grass to watch. The afternoon sun felt warm on her back, and the sky overhead was bright blue. It was a beautiful day; for a second she was tempted to change her mind.

But just then she saw a girl with a red baseball cap take a powerful swing with her bat. There was a loud *crack*! and the softball soared into the air.

Forget about it, Megan decided. There was no way she was playing with these kids. She'd make a fool of herself for sure.

As the players began to take the field, Megan heard Mark ask Alison if she wanted to pitch.

"Sure," Alison replied. She had a fierce expression on

her face. "The Wildcats are toast."

"Now I'm *really* glad that I'm not playing, Ali," Megan called out, laughing. "I wouldn't want you to get mad at me when I made all the outs!"

To Megan's surprise, Alison didn't laugh. "It's just a game, Megan," she said, sounding impatient. "You don't have to do *everything* perfectly, you know." Before Megan could say anything, Alison jogged away to take her place on the mound.

Megan stared after her, her cheeks flaming. I can't believe Alison just said that to me, she muttered to herself.

I don't think I have to be perfect at everything. Besides, Alison is so good at sports, she has no idea what it feels like to strike out or make a team lose.

"Hey, Megan!" Alison yelled a few minutes later when the team ran in from the field. "What did you think of Keisha's all–star play?"

But Megan didn't reply. Instead she stood up and stalked away from the field.

"Megan?" Alison called. "Are you okay?"

"I'm fine," Megan snapped without looking back. Then she hopped on her bike and pedaled home, alone.

"So how was your day, sweetie pie?" Mrs. Ryder asked

at dinner.

"Okay, I guess," Megan replied flatly.

"That doesn't sound very enthusiastic," her mother observed.

"It's no big deal," Megan said, pushing the food around with a fork. "But Alison said something today that's still bothering me."

"Alison?" Mrs. Ryder looked surprised. "What did she say?"

"She told me that I don't have to do *everything* perfectly," Megan said, imitating Alison's tone.

Mrs. Ryder listened to the story. "It sounds like she was calling you a perfectionist."

"I'm not a perfectionist, Mom," Megan insisted.

"Well, you're very hard on yourself, Megs," her mother replied. "And you do expect to always be the best, especially in school."

Megan sighed, suddenly wishing that she'd never brought the topic up. "Can we please talk about something else?"

"Sure. I actually have some exciting news—I've been asked to give a speech at a big legal conference."

"That's good," Megan said with a sigh.

Mrs. Ryder laughed. "There's more. I haven't told you the best part—the conference is being held in

Washington, D.C."

"Washington, D.C.!" Megan echoed. "That's near Grandma and Grandpa Ryder's house! Can I go with you?"

Her mother nodded. "When I told Grandma that we were coming, she suggested you bring along a friend."

"Yes!" Megan cried. Her grandparents were lots of fun and they lived in a pretty rural town that was near a riding stable and a lake with paddleboats. Megan would love to take one of her friends there and show her around.

Megan leaned over and gave her mother a big hug.

"You're the best, Mom."

Mrs. Ryder's green eyes twinkled. "I hope the lawyers in my audience agree with you," she said.

As soon as Megan finished clearing the dishes from the table, she ran to the phone. She couldn't wait to call Keisha and invite her on the trip.

Chapter TWO

THE SEQUINED LEOTARD

ello?" a young child said into the phone.

Megan smiled. It was Keisha's five-year-old sister, Ashley. One of her favorite things to do lately was answer the phone. "Hi, Ashley. It's Megan. May I please speak with Keisha?"

Megan heard Ashley breathing loudly into the phone for a second before the receiver fell to the floor with a loud *crash*. "Mom, is Keisha allowed to talk to Megan?" Megan heard Ashley ask. "Of course I'm allowed to talk to her!" she heard Keisha reply in an exasperated tone.

"You are *so* lucky you don't have any younger brothers and sisters," Keisha said to Megan a second later. "Ashley is driving me crazy!"

Megan laughed. "I can see why!"

"I tried to call you earlier," Keisha said, changing the subject. "Were you upset about something this afternoon?"

"No," Megan lied. "Actually, I've got great news. How would you like to come to my grandparents' house for a few days?"

"That sounds great," Keisha answered. "When?"

"My mom says we'll leave the Friday before Memorial Day and come back on Monday night. We can go horseback riding, and—"

"I can't," Keisha interrupted, sounding disappointed. "We're going to the beach that weekend."

Megan felt the excitement draining out of her like air seeping out of a balloon. But by the time she and Keisha hung up, she had perked up—maybe Heather could go. Eagerly, she dialed the number. But Heather said that her parents were making her go to a family reunion that weekend.

"Rats." Megan sighed loudly as she put down the receiver.

Mrs. Ryder looked up from the kitchen table. "What's

wrong?" she asked sympathetically.

Megan explained about Keisha and Heather.

"Why don't you try Alison?" her mother suggested.

"I don't think so, Mom," Megan said. Just then the phone rang, startling her.

"Megan?" It was Alison. "Are you sure you're not angry with us for playing softball this afternoon?"

Megan's face flushed. "No, I'm not angry about that..."

"What's wrong, then?" Alison persisted.

Megan hesitated. She wanted to explain that Alison had hurt her feelings, but she couldn't get the words out. Instead, without thinking, she blurted out, "Actually, I was just about to call you, Ali. I was wondering if you wanted..."

As soon as Alison heard about the trip, she let out a whoop. "That sounds great, Megan! My parents both have to work that weekend, so my family isn't going anywhere."

"Good," Megan said, trying to sound cheerful. "There's

lots to do at my grandparents' house. We can ride the paddleboats and play in the woods, and—"

"Hey!" Alison cut in. "Don't your grandparents live near that big amusement park, the one with the Tornado Twister roller coaster?"

"You mean Fun City?" Megan asked.

"Yes, that's it," Alison said. "Maybe we can go there instead!"

"Uh—maybe," Megan said hesitantly.

While Alison went on and on about how much fun it would be to ride the Tornado Twister, Megan remained quiet. Inside, she felt herself getting angry all over again. Doesn't Alison remember that I don't really like scary rides or amusement parks? she said to herself.

"So it's all set?" Mrs. Ryder asked cheerfully when Megan hung up the phone. "Alison is coming?"

"Yes....It's all set," Megan mumbled.

As she headed up the stairs, Megan wished she could take back her invitation.

The next day, Megan couldn't stop thinking about the situation with Alison. She

18

decided a visit with her neighbor might take her mind off her problems.

Megan and her three best friends had started visiting Ellie shortly after she moved back into the neighborhood. Her amazing Victorian house was filled with fascinating books, pictures, and souvenirs from her trips around the world. The four girls loved hearing the older woman's stories about all the interesting places she'd visited. And they formed the Magic Attic Club after they discovered the wonderful adventures that awaited them in Ellie's attic.

"Oh, Megan," Ellie Goodwin said as she came to the door. "What a nice surprise."

"Hi, Ellie," Megan said. "May I come in?"

"Of course, my dear, *entrez*," Ellie said with a dramatic flourish.

Ellie's silver hair was pulled back in a French braid and she wore a cream-colored silk dress with a strand of antique gold beads. A delicious aroma filled the air.

"Mmmmmm," Megan said, inhaling deeply.

"*Coq au vin*," Ellie answered.

"What's a cocoa van?" asked Megan.

"It's chicken cooked in wine, and it's very tasty. I'm making it for an old friend who's coming for dinner."

Suddenly Megan felt embarrassed. She was about to ask if she should come back another time when Ellie smiled and put a hand on her shoulder.

"Your timing couldn't be better, Megan. Dorothy won't be here for another few minutes, and I've got plenty more to do in the kitchen." With that, Ellie gently spun Megan around and pointed her in the direction of the table where the small silver box rested. "Have fun, my dear," she added softly.

"Thanks, Ellie," Megan said. She quickly reached inside the box and scooped up the gold scrolled key. Then she dashed up to the second floor and unlocked the door to the attic.

A feeling of excitement washed over Megan as soon as she entered the familiar room. A worn oriental rug covered the honey-colored floorboards, and an antique mahogany wardrobe stood against one wall. Nearby was a desk where bundles of old letters and photos were stored. But Megan's eyes went right to the black leather and oak steamer trunk across the room.

Megan pulled the satin cord on the overhead light. Outside dusk was starting to fall and the scent of freshly cut grass drifted in through an open window. As Megan knelt in front of the trunk and lifted the lid, a sparkle caught her eye. On top of a pile of colorful clothing lay a brand new leotard.

Megan held it up. It was made of sparkly gold fabric

trimmed with bands of red and blue sequins. It reminded her of the ones that she'd seen gymnasts wearing during the Olympics. She could still picture the talented athletes vaulting through the air and performing their dazzling routines on the balance beam.

Wouldn't it be incredible to actually...

Before she had even completed the thought, Megan kicked off her shoes and pulled on the leotard. She reached back into the trunk and found a gold-colored scrunchie for her hair. Then she hurried over to the tall, gilt-edged mirror.

I look like a real gymnast, she thought. This is so cool. She reached one of her arms back and grabbed an ankle, the way she'd seen athletes on TV do it on the balance beam.

The walls of Ellie's attic began to fade.

When everything came into focus again, Megan found herself in the same position. But now she was poised on a real balance beam.

Chapter Three

THE
FLAMINGOS

 egan!" someone called sharply.

Megan was so startled that her bare feet nearly slipped off the narrow beam.

A tall, athletic-looking woman across the room was looking at Megan, and so was a group of about six girls. One of them had on a gold leotard that matched Megan's; the others all wore different colors.

"Please dismount and join us for the team meeting, Megan," the woman went on.

Megan felt a knot form inside her stomach. How was she supposed to get off this thing without looking like a total klutz? But before she knew what she was doing, she had leaped off the beam and landed gracefully on the thick mat that covered the polished wood floor. She hurried across the gym and joined the other girls.

"Okay, Flamingos. We're going to start our workout, I promise," the woman said. Megan figured she must be the coach. "But first I want to go over a few things."

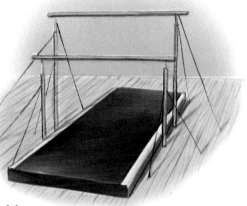

While the woman talked, Megan tried to get her bearings. She had obviously arrived inside a gym, and she was pretty sure that she was on a gymnastics team called the Flamingos. Scattered around the room were several pieces of equipment—the high beam where Megan had just been standing; two low practice beams set up on the floor; thick, knotted ropes hanging from the ceiling; a horse for vaulting; and two sets of uneven parallel bars. There was no equipment in one corner of the room, but the floor was completely covered with thick blue mats. That must be where the gymnasts practiced their floor exercises, Megan thought. Across the room were bleachers for spectators.

Megan snapped back to attention when she heard the words "important competition."

"I want you guys here tomorrow morning at eight sharp," the woman was saying. "The Invitational begins officially at ten o'clock."

"Yea!" cheered a girl in a light blue leotard, her long, black hair pulled back in a ponytail. "We're going to cream the Cougars," she added.

"Greta?" A petite girl raised her hand. "How many teams are coming to the Invitational?"

"Five teams besides the Flamingos, Samantha," the coach answered. "And I'm sure I don't have to remind you, the first–place team will go to the Regional competition next weekend,"

"The Regional is even more important than the Invitational," the youngest-looking girl chimed in. "Samantha told me that the best teams from the whole state will be there." Megan thought the girl looked a lot like Samantha; they were probably sisters.

"That's right, Jessica," Greta said. "But we don't have to worry about that for another week. For now, let's just concentrate on performing our best tomorrow. Any more questions?"

A redheaded girl wearing a bright blue leotard cleared her throat. "I have a question," she began.

"Kelly?"

Megan saw a glimmer of mischief in Kelly's eyes. "What's the best way to catch a squirrel?"

Samantha and Jessica giggled.

"I give up, Kelly," Jessica said. "What?"

"Climb a tree and act like a nut!" Kelly told her. Everybody laughed at the dumb joke, except the girl with the long black ponytail.

"Oh, grow up, Kelly," she snapped. "You act like a five–year–old sometimes."

"I'm just trying to have some fun, Mariah," Kelly replied evenly.

"Okay, guys." The coach held up a hand, then went on discussing the meet. Megan felt herself growing nervous. How in the world was she going to compete in the meet when she could barely do a handspring or a cartwheel!

Sunflowers   Flamingos

Finally, the coach started the girls on their workout. "Let's warm up by jogging around the gym. Then we'll do our stretches," she instructed.

26

Megan stood up and fell in line behind the other girls. It wasn't until they ran briskly around the gym that she noticed the colorful felt banners that decorated the walls. Several had team names printed on them, such as FLAMINGOS and SUNFLOWERS. Over one of the doors another sign read JOIN MRS. COLBY'S GYM FOR FUN AND FITNESS.

So that's where I am, Megan said to herself, Mrs. Colby's Gym.

After the warmup, the coach divided the team into groups.

"Samantha and Jessica—start on the floor, then rotate onto the unevens. Robin, Kelly, and Brooke—go to vaulting. Megan and Mariah, you're on the beam first. I want to see you two working on your jumps and landings, okay?"

"Okay," Megan said, trying to sound confident. But as she followed Mariah to the balance beam, she could feel the butterflies fluttering in her stomach again. She hoped no one would see how shaky she was.

To her relief, Mariah mounted the beam first. She extended her arms to the sides and walked along the beam, smoothly "dipping" one foot at a time below the beam. The movement looked easy, but Megan knew it took a lot of balance and coordination. Mariah was obviously a very talented gymnast.

"Your routine looked terrific," Megan said.

"Thanks." Mariah grinned and took a little bow. "The beam's not my best event, but I've improved a lot since I joined the Flamingos and started working with Greta."

Next it was Megan's turn. As she stepped toward the beam, she took a deep breath, trying to steady herself. Then quickly, before she could lose her nerve, she bounced off the springboard. To her surprise, she instantly mounted the beam.

Wow, Megan thought as her body went into a handstand, this is amazing! Her body seemed to know just what moves to make, and she had never felt so light or flexible.

Omigosh, she was thinking, I'm really a gymnast!

Chapter

Four

IN THE
LOCKER ROOM

 egan spent the rest of the workout session practicing the other three gymnastics events:uneven parallel bars, vaulting, and the floor exercises. She began her turn on the uneven parallel bars by dusting her hands with chalk, just as she'd seen the other girls do. Then she pulled on a pair of hand guards. Again, she mounted the apparatus with a difficult movement that Greta called a pike glide kip. For the next few minutes, she practiced several of the circles and hangs that she would have to perform at the competition the next day.

Even though she didn't feel as confident on the bars as she did on the balance beam, Megan quickly realized why it was the favorite of so many gymnasts. It was thrilling to be able to swing your body through the air and wrap it around the bars.

Megan and Mariah started their floor exercise at the same time. Kelly was still working on the mats as they approached.

"Greta said you're supposed to be working on the beam now," Mariah said in an exasperated tone.

"I know," Kelly retorted.

As the girls glared at each other, Megan just stared at the mat, embarrassed. She had noticed the tension between the two girls during the team meeting; now it was even more apparent.

"I can't believe that girl is on our team," Mariah said when Kelly finally walked away.

"What do you mean?" Megan asked.

"She's not very talented," Mariah went on. "I have no idea why Greta even let her join."

"I watched Kelly practicing her floor routine," Megan said, trying to be diplomatic. "I thought she was pretty good."

"She's okay on the floor," Mariah replied. "But she totally lacks confidence on the beam. Plus, this is her first competition." She shot a nasty look in Kelly's direction.

"I know how much you like to chat, girls,"Greta interrupted, giving Megan and Mariah a pointed glance. "But please save it for the locker room."

"Sorry," Megan said, blushing. She had just arrived; the last thing she needed was to get in trouble with the coach.

Later in the locker room, the din of metal doors clanging and girls laughing filled the air. A group of younger kids had arrived for practice, and now all the tiny "Parakeets" were talking to one another while they changed into their leotards.

Megan glanced around at the walls of red lockers, trying to figure out which one belonged to her. Suddenly, she realized that someone was trying to get her attention.

"Earth to Megan," Kelly said, snapping her fingers in front of Megan's face.

"Oh hi," Megan said, startled.

Kelly grinned. "Were you in a trance, or daydreaming about something?"

Megan just smiled and shook her head.

"Come on, let's get changed before we miss our rides home," Kelly said. "Greta's driving you back to her house, right?"

Megan nodded. Judging by what Mariah had said earlier, Megan and Brooke were both staying at Greta's house while they trained for the competition.

Megan followed Kelly to the next row of lockers. To her relief, one of them was marked with her name. She swung open the door. Inside there was a water bottle and a neatly folded white satin warm-up jacket with red and blue trim that matched her leotard.As she pulled on a pair of sweat pants and chatted with Kelly, she saw Mariah striding purposefully toward them. Mariah turned to Kelly, her hands on her hips.

"You'd better not blow it tomorrow, Kelly," she warned the redhead.

"I'm not planning to," Kelly said coldly.

"Well, if I were you, I wouldn't take any chances,"

Mariah went on. "I'd quit the team before I ruined it for everyone else." With that, she whirled around and stalked off in the other direction.

Megan felt her mouth drop open. How could Mariah be so nasty, she wondered, especially when she knows it's Kelly's first big competition.

Kelly's cheeks had turned a bright pink. She shot to her feet and immediately started twirling the combination on her locker. "So," she said with a forced laugh, "wasn't it nice of Mariah to drop by and wish me luck in the Invitational?"

"Don't pay any attention to her," Megan replied quickly.

Kelly waved a hand dismissively. "I've already forgotten about it," she said cheerfully. "Who cares what she says?"

"Good for you," Megan said, surprised. If Mariah had treated *her* that way . . .

"I'm sure you'll do great tomorrow," Megan assured her.

"That's right," Kelly agreed. "I'll probably score a perfect ten. Well, maybe not that high..." she added with a grin. "But at least a nine point eight." Then she changed the subject. "Did I tell you that my parents are taking me out to lunch at a Mexican restaurant after the meet?"

Megan shook her head. She decided that she liked Kelly a lot. She was fun and friendly. And easygoing, too. To Megan's relief, it seemed Kelly had forgotten about Mariah's comments in no time at all.

Chapter

Five

THE
INVITATIONAL
BEGINS

ntroducing…" The announcer paused as a group of girls dressed in white leotards with blue and gold stripes stood and waved to the crowd. "…the Cougars from the Country Gym!" Enthusiastic applause rose from the bleachers.

Megan's heart pounded as she clapped for the Cougars, too. She had watched them during the morning warm–up session. There were several very accomplished gymnasts on their team, and they would be hard to beat.

When the announcer introduced the Flamingos, Megan and her teammates stood and waved to the crowd. They all wore the same leotard that Megan had found in Ellie's trunk. They looked really cool and professional.

A second later, the floor of the gym bustled with activity as the gymnasts from each team took their places for their first event. As the Flamingos headed toward the unevens, Megan tried to dry her palms without being noticed. For once, though, she was more excited than scared or nervous.

The girls gathered around Greta and Mrs. Colby.

"You're up first, Samantha," Greta said, consulting her clipboard. "Mariah, you're next, then Jessica, Kelly, Robin, Brooke, and Megan. That's the order we'll follow all day—okay, girls?"

They all nodded. Then Greta turned to Kelly. "Did you go over your routine on the beam this morning?" she asked.

Kelly grinned. "Aye, Captain," she replied, snapping a quick military salute. "I'm ready to win a gold."

"Good." Greta smiled back. "That's the attitude I like to see."

Megan watched Samantha pull on her hand guards and chalk up. A minute later, an official waved a small flag. As Samantha hurried toward the uneven bars and mounted, music started up across the room, where the floor exercises were being held.

An excited shiver crept up Megan's spine. The Invitational at Mrs. Colby's Gym had officially begun!

"Are we still in second place?" Brooke whispered to Megan. The team was sitting on the bench; the meet was almost over. The Flamingos had only one more event to complete—the beam.

"I think so," Megan murmured, checking the scoreboard. The Cougars were finished for the day, and the judges had just posted their final team score. Megan was surprised to see that they hadn't done very well in vaulting, and that their overall score was lower than she had expected.

Megan gripped Brooke's arm. "You know what? If we all do well on the beam, we might still have a shot at first place."

"Really?" Brooke said eagerly.

"I wouldn't get my hopes up, girls," Mariah piped up. She cocked her head toward the end of the row, where Kelly sat. "We have you-know-who on our team, remember?"

"Leave Kelly alone!" Megan snapped before she could stop herself.

"I just want to win, Megan," Mariah retorted defensively. "There's nothing wrong with that. Even *you* should understand that."

Megan let the subject drop as an official gave Samantha the signal. But she couldn't help glancing toward the end of the bench. Kelly was chewing her lower lip and staring straight ahead.

Please don't blow it, Kelly, Megan said to herself. Immediately, she felt a stab of guilt. Am I worried about her performance, she wondered, or mine? What if I suddenly turn into Megan the Klutz again? What if...

By the time Kelly's turn came, Megan was a nervous wreck. Samantha, Mariah, and Jessica had all gotten high scores, and the Flamingos had a slight lead over the Cougars. If they continued to perform well, they could win the gold medal.

In the stands, the crowd had gone completely quiet. All of the other events had ended for the day. Across the room, the Cougars stood together in their blue warmups, their eyes glued on Kelly as she prepared for her first difficult move, a straight-leg leap.

Kelly mounted nicely, then went into a cartwheel. For the rest of the routine, Megan didn't move a muscle, even though she saw Kelly make several mistakes—she had arched her back during a handstand, and she'd omitted

one of her jumps—but so far none of those things spelled disaster.

Then Kelly began her dismount. As she went into a cartwheel, she misjudged where to place her hand.

Megan heard herself gasp as Kelly tumbled off the beam and onto the floor.

It's over, Megan thought, glancing at the scoreboard. Luckily, Kelly hadn't been hurt, and she'd gotten right back on the beam. But together with her other errors, the fall had cost her—and her teammates—a big deduction. Her final score was only 7.9.

Megan was the last Flamingo on the beam.

She stepped up to the springboard, then closed her eyes for a moment, trying to shut out

7.9 8.6 9.0 9.8

everything but her routine: backward swing turn…cross handstand…forward coupe…

Suddenly Greta touched her shoulder—it was time to start. Megan nodded, then took a deep breath before bouncing off the springboard. A second later, her bare feet gripped the beam.

Megan pivoted, then went into a cross handstand. She held it for one second, then dropped down, preparing for the first jump.

Ninety seconds seemed to go by in no time at all. Once again Megan's body instinctively knew every movement and skill. As she began her dismount—a cartwheel, handstand, then quarter turn—she felt her heart soar. She knew she had done a very strong routine.

Megan was beaming as she landed and threw open her arms. The crowd cheered loudly. Happily, she waved back, then hurried over to the bench.

"You nailed it, Megan!" Brooke and Robin called out.

"Congratulations!" Samantha cried, jumping up and down and hugging her. As Megan reached for her water bottle, she heard Brooke gasp.

"Omigosh!"

"What?" Megan said nervously. When she looked up, she saw for herself. Her score was 9.8—the highest score of the day!

Just then, the announcer's voice boomed into the megaphone.

"Congratulations to Mrs. Colby's Flamingos! You've won the gold trophy in the team competition!"

The gym thundered with applause and cheers. Mariah hugged Megan hard. "Did you hear that?" she shouted.

"We're going to the Regional!"

Megan stood grinning at the scoreboard. But as she scanned the crowded floor, her smile slowly faded.

"Greta?" she asked. "Have you seen Kelly?"

"She left right after her routine," Greta replied. "Something about having to baby-sit her sisters."

Everyone around Megan—teammates and their parents—was chattering happily about going to the Regional.

Everyone but Megan.

Chapter
Six

MEGAN GIVES ADVICE

s soon as the awards had been given out, Megan hurried into Mrs. Colby's office. The tiny office was decorated with pretty furniture and a colorful braided rug, and the walls were lined with glass cases filled with trophies and medals. Megan quickly found a list of the Flamingos' phone numbers tacked to a bulletin board. She sat on the floor and dialed Kelly's number.

"Hi, Kelly? It's Megan. I was just calling to see if you're okay."

Kelly hesitated. "Of course I'm okay. Why?"

"You left the meet right after your routine—" Megan started.

"My mom had a doctor's appointment this afternoon," Kelly cut in. "I had to get home to baby-sit my sisters."

"I just thought...I guess I thought that you were upset," Megan explained.

"About my routine?" Kelly laughed loudly. "Don't be silly, Megan. I was just demonstrating my skills—you know, in falling *off* the beam."

"Oh." Megan laughed uncertainly. "Well, guess what?" she went on. "We won the meet."

"What?" Kelly sounded shocked. "We won?"

"Yes. Can you believe it? We're going to the Regional."

"That's so great, Megan," Kelly said. "And you must be happy. It's all because of you."

"Everyone did her best," Megan said quickly. "In fact—" But before she could tell her any details, Kelly interrupted again.

"Listen, I'd better go before...I think my sisters are about to use Mom's good china for their tea party. See you around," she added abruptly. There was a loud *click* and the line went dead.

What was that about? Megan thought. What about going to lunch with her mom and dad? Megan felt sure

that Kelly had lied about having to baby-sit, so that no one would know how upset she was.

Megan sat holding the receiver for a few minutes, then hung up and made her way back to the gym floor. The rest of her teammates and most of their parents were gathered in the center. Greta was pouring ginger ale into plastic champagne glasses, and Mrs. Colby was filling bowls with popcorn and pretzels.

Suddenly Brooke said enthusiastically, "Let's hear it for Megan, the star of the team!" She raised her glass in a toast."Hip, hip, hooray!" Everyone else joined in.

Mrs. Colby chuckled at the doubtful expression on Megan's face. "Don't be modest, Megan," she said warmly, putting an arm around her. "You did a great job today."

"You sure did," Mariah chimed in. "We won because of you!"

A big smile crossed Megan's face. Thanks to Ellie's mirror, she had become the best gymnast on the team.

That week, all Megan could think about was getting ready for the Regional competition. The Flamingos practiced on their usual three days—Monday, Wednesday, and Thursday— and Greta added an extra session for Friday afternoon, the day before the meet.

When Megan walked into the gym on Friday, she was surprised to see Kelly already practicing. There was a look of fierce concentration on her face.

Kelly had looked unsteady on the beam all week, and Megan couldn't help noticing that it was true again today. Her jumps looked uncertain and sloppy, and once or twice she nearly fell.

Kelly dismounted, landing face to face with Megan. She looked embarrassed for a second, but quickly recovered.

"Hey," she said, flashing a friendly smile, "I'm glad you were able to catch my routine one last time. I'll probably be heading off to the World Championships any day now."

Megan smiled. "Your handstand looked great," Megan said, trying to encourage her. "Once you get your confidence back, I bet your jumps will improve too."

"I don't know," Kelly said, suddenly sounding serious. "I'm starting to agree with Mariah—I'm hopeless." Then she quickly turned around and remounted the beam.

For the next hour and a half, Megan didn't have time to think about Kelly's problems. Greta worked the team members hard, trying to get them ready for the big meet.

Megan had just rotated to the vaulting horse for the second time when Mrs. Colby entered the gym, carrying a big bag.

"Okay, guys," Greta called suddenly. "We've finished our workout for this afternoon."

"Good," Brooke said. "I'm exhausted."

Greta waved everyone over to the area where the blue mats were spread out on the floor. "Gather round, guys. Mrs. Colby has a surprise for you."

"A surprise!" Jessica echoed. "What is it?"

"You'll see in a minute," Mrs. Colby replied, her brown eyes twinkling.

Megan watched with curiosity as Mrs. Colby reached

into the bag and pulled
something out.

"New gym bags!"
Brooke exclaimed.

"Cool!" Robin said as
Mrs. Colby held up the
sleek-looking bags for
everyone to see. "I bet they'll come in handy."

"They're a perfect match for our leotards and jackets,"
Samantha said.

"I have something else," Mrs. Colby murmured,
rummaging around inside the bag. This time she pulled
out several pairs of satiny white pants.

"Wow!" Jessica slipped the smallest pair over her legs,
snapping the elastic waistband a couple of times. "Now
we'll look like real pros."

"Just what I was thinking," Mrs. Colby said, smiling.
"That's why I wanted to give these to you before the
Regional."

"Speaking of the Regional," Greta added. "I want
everyone to get a good night's rest tonight. The meet is
very important, and we want you to do your best
tomorrow, but we also want you to be relaxed and
have fun."

"Do you think we'll win?" Jessica piped up suddenly.

"Not with Kelly on our team," Mariah murmured.

Megan flinched. Mariah had made the comment in a low voice, but it was loud enough for everyone to hear.

"That's enough, Mariah," Mrs. Colby said sharply. There was a spark of anger in her eyes. "I will not tolerate that kind of remark from anyone in my gym. Do you understand?"

"Sorry, Mrs. Colby."

Megan looked around. Kelly was staring down at the blue mat, intently running her toes back and forth over a seam that had been stitched up with heavy thread.

"As for your question, Jessica," Mrs. Colby went on, "I don't know if we'll win. The ten best teams in the state will be there, and the competition will be intense, but I've learned that winning isn't what's most important."

Jessica wrinkled her nose. "Then what is?"

Everyone laughed, but Mrs. Colby's answer was a serious one. "Being a part of the team and doing your best," she said. "I hope that's something you learn for yourselves tomorrow."

"All right, Flamingos," Greta said. "We'll see you bright and early."

In the parking lot, waiting for her ride, Megan spotted Kelly standing alone. "Aren't you excited about tomorrow?" Megan asked.

"I'm quitting the team," Kelly said.

"But...you can't," Megan blurted out.

"Why not?" Kelly whirled to face her. "I'm sure that Greta and Mrs. Colby can find someone better to take my place. That would certainly make Mariah happy."

"Come on, Kelly," Megan urged her. "At least come to the Regional and give it another try."

"No." Kelly shook her head. Then her tone seemed to soften. "Look, Megan. I know you're trying to cheer me up, but there's no way you can understand how I feel. You're the best gymnast on the team and you have no idea how it feels to be the worst one."

Yes I do! Megan wanted to shout. But she couldn't. Instead she remembered what her mother had told her. "Kelly," she began, "everybody can't be the best—that's not what makes a team. Without you, there are no Flamingos at all, not even in *last* place."

"Trust me," Megan went on. "All you have to do is try your best. No one can ask for anything more."

Chapter

Seven

HONK FOR THE FLAMINGOS!

 hen Megan arrived at the gym parking lot the next morning with Greta and Brooke, it was still dark outside. Samantha and Jessica were already waiting.

"Boy, is it cold," Samantha said, shivering.

"Boy, is it *early*," Jessica chimed in.

When Mariah arrived, there was a wash of pink in the sky where the sun was starting to rise. Robin arrived a moment later. Megan glanced toward the street and frowned.

"Maybe Kelly overslept, Megan," Brooke said softly.

"Maybe," Megan said doubtfully. She felt sure her little speech hadn't worked.

"We might have to forfeit if Kelly doesn't show up," Robin said. "Without her, we won't have enough gymnasts to compete."

Just then, Greta came out of the gym.

"I can't believe this!" Mariah wailed loudly. "First, Kelly practically makes us lose at the Invitational. Now she quits the day before the Regional so it's too late for us to get anyone else!"

"Mariah, please," Greta said. "Complaining about Kelly isn't going to do us any good. Mrs. Colby will be here any minute. We'll drive to the arena and tell the judges what happened. Maybe they'll still let us compete."

Megan paced along the curb while they all waited for Mrs. Colby. Nobody said another word until Robin pointed to a van turning into the parking lot.

Megan had seen it parked outside the gym before, but today it looked completely different. It had been painted a pale pink—to match the color of real flamingos—and on one side, Mrs. Colby had hung a banner that read, HONK FOR MRS. COLBY'S FLAMINGOS!

Mrs. Colby beeped the horn and waved, but nobody waved back. "Why the long faces?" she asked, rolling down the window.

Greta told her about Kelly.

Mrs. Colby's smile faded for a second, but then her face brightened again. "Climb aboard, Flamingos," she said. "Maybe there's hope yet."

When the team arrived at the arena, Greta ushered them toward the locker room. "I'll track down the judges. You've got ten minutes to get the kinks out, then ten to warm up on the equipment," she told them.

The girls changed, then followed Mrs. Colby into the gym. The bleachers were already filling with spectators. Many were holding up signs printed with the teams' names. A group of parents started cheering "Let's go, Flamingos!" as the team walked onto the floor.

Megan sat on a mat and began to stretch her muscles, but she couldn't concentrate. All she could think about was Greta and what was taking her so long.

Halfway through their warm-up on the equipment, the coach appeared.

"I'm sorry, girls," Greta said. "The judges wanted to help us, but they have to follow the rules. Every team has to have seven gymnasts."

"But—" Jessica started.

Greta held up a hand. "I tried my best, you guys," she said. "But believe me, there isn't anything more we can do."

Mrs. Colby looked upset, too. "Come on, girls," she said. "As long as we're here, we can find seats in the stands and watch."

"Watch?" Mariah blurted out. "But I don't want to watch. I want to compete."

"We all want to compete, Mariah," Brooke snapped. "But Greta just finished telling us that we're not allowed. And you know something else?" she went on, gathering steam. "It's your fault!"

"My fault?" Mariah echoed. "It's Kelly's fault!"

"Okay, girls," Mrs. Colby intervened. "Arguing isn't going to change anything. And it's certainly not helping anyone's spirits right now."

As Megan dropped down on the bleachers, her eye caught a flash of red and blue halfway across the gym. She squinted to see better. A red-haired girl with sequins and stars on her warm-up jacket was hurrying toward them.

In an instant, Megan was on her feet. "Kelly!" she shouted, waving frantically. The others had spotted their teammate, too. They all jumped up and raced toward her.

Jessica threw her arms around Kelly in a big hug. "I can't believe you're here!" she exclaimed.

Mariah hung back for a second, then approached Kelly too. Megan heard her mumble, "I'm glad you came, Kelly."

"Me, too," Kelly said. "My mom and I just got here."

Megan caught her friend's eye and they smiled at each other. Greta gave a happy nod, then rushed over to tell the judges that the team was complete.

As the seven members of the Flamingos hurried back onto the floor, Mrs. Colby put her arm around Kelly's shoulder and whispered urgently into her ear.

"What's the matter?" Megan asked.

"Kelly hasn't had a chance to warm up," said Samantha. "She could really hurt herself if she's not careful."

"Yeah, we're still going to lose on account of Kelly," Mariah muttered, sounding genuinely upset.

The Flamingos' next–to–last event was the balance beam. It was probably too late for the them to place first or second, but they might still have a chance to come in third.

Four of the girls—including Kelly—had turned in solid

performances. Samantha was nearly finished with her routine. Next it would be Megan's turn.

Megan closed her eyes and tried to focus. As Samantha dismounted, Megan heard someone call her name softly.

She looked along the bench and saw Kelly flash her a thumbs-up. Megan nodded her thanks.

As she approached the beam, a rock–and–roll song started up as another gymnast began her floor exercise. Megan inhaled deeply, but she wasn't really nervous. The beam, and her routine, had become as familiar to her as walking.

Megan stood poised for a moment, and then, with a powerful jump, she mounted the beam. She went into her handstand, held it, and dropped down. And then effortlessly, she spun into a graceful arabesque.

A moment later, it was over. As Megan landed her dismount and threw open her arms to the crowd, the cavernous gym seemed to explode with cheers.

"Great job, Flamingos!" Greta said with a broad smile. The awards ceremony had just ended.

"I'll say," Mrs. Colby chimed in. She held up the gleaming trophy for everyone to see. "I'm so proud of you girls!"

Megan beamed, clapping happily with the other girls.

"We were great, weren't we?" Brooke said.

"I guess we won't get a trophy for being modest though, will we?" Kelly joked.

Everyone laughed—even Mariah, Megan noticed.

"Let's pack up and go celebrate," Mrs. Colby said.

Megan followed her teammates into the locker room. She had just finished pulling on her warm–up pants when she noticed Kelly coming toward her.

"Thanks, Megan," she said, giving her a hug. "You're the best."

Megan just smiled back. What a wonderful adventure, she thought. She had enjoyed nearly every minute of it. But now that the competition was over, she knew that it was time for her to go home.

Megan stood in front of one of the wall mirrors. She smiled as she stared at her reflection in the glass, and the next thing she knew, she was back in Ellie's attic.

chapter Eight

BACK
HOME

egan smoothed out the wrinkles in the white leotard and carefully placed it back in Ellie's trunk. She heard excited barking from Monty downstairs, followed by peals of laughter.

Who is Ellie talking to? Megan wondered. As she locked the attic and headed downstairs, she remembered Ellie's mentioning that a friend was coming for dinner.

Megan followed the voices to the sitting room, where she found Ellie and a woman with short salt–and–pepper hair. The two women were both laughing so hard that they didn't notice Megan standing in the doorway until she cleared her throat.

"Excuse me, Ellie," Megan said.

"Megan! Come in and meet Dorothy, my old friend from high school."

"Hello Megan." The woman stood up to shake Megan's hand.

Megan smiled back. "Have you two really been friends since high school?"

"Well, we weren't friends right from the start," Dorothy said. "Were we, Ellie?"

"Absolutely not," Ellie said, shaking her head. "When Dorothy and I first met, we disagreed about everything."

"What do you mean?" Dorothy said, putting a hand on her hip and pretending to be indignant. "We still disagree about nearly everything!"

Ellie burst into fresh laughter. "That's true," she admitted. "But look at us Megan. We're still very close friends!"

Megan stayed for a few more minutes, then politely said good-bye. As she closed Ellie's front door, she could still hear the women's laughter. Megan smiled. The two of them seemed to have as much fun together as she and her three best friends.

"Hi, Megan!" Mrs. Ryder called as Megan opened the door.

"Mom?" Surprised, Megan went into the living room. "What are you doing home? I thought you were staying late at the office tonight to work on your speech for the conference."

"That was my plan," Mrs. Ryder said. Megan watched her mother pace back and forth across the carpet. "But I'm so nervous about speaking in front of a large group," she confessed, "that I can't write a word."

"You?" Megan said, astonished. She couldn't remember another time when her confident, successful mother had admitted that she was nervous about something. "But you always give speeches, Mom."

"And I always get nervous," her mother replied. "All I can think about is, what if it's not as good as the other speakers? Or what if I put everybody to sleep?"

"You sound just like me, Mom!" Megan exclaimed. "No wonder I'm such a perfectionist!"

Mrs. Ryder laughed and shook her head. "Maybe we both need Alison to tell us to lighten up sometimes," she said.

Megan laughed, too. For the first time since she'd gone up to Ellie's attic, she found herself thinking about what Alison had said to her on the softball field. Just a few hours earlier the remark had stung a lot, but now, to Megan's surprise, the hurt feelings were gone.

Megan helped her mother write and rehearse her speech for a little while. Then she went into the kitchen to call Alison. Their trip to Maryland was just ten days away, and they had a lot of plans to make together.

Diary

Dear Diary,

   I'm sorry that I haven't written in a while, but I've been really busy. Boy, do I have a lot to tell you about!

   First of all, I had the most fabulous adventure in Ellie's attic. I became a member of the Flamingos, a competitive gymnastics team. It was a lot of fun. I loved being able to perform all kinds of turns and jumps on the beam. Plus, I won two awards, and our team won a trophy in the Regional competition for coming in third.

   It's funny, but after being the best gymnast on the Flamingos, I've realized something. It's fun to win medals and trophies and everything, but you don't have to come in first to have fun and be a part of a team. It was hard to admit it to myself, but Alison was right. I *am* a perfectionist sometimes. I hope I can remember to lighten up the next time that

Alison's brother asks me to play softball and be

willing to give it a try!

    Alison and I had lots of fun in Maryland. It was

great to see Grandma and Grandpa Ryder, and

Alison and I got along really well. We went

horseback riding and rode the paddleboats, and we

went to Fun City, too. Alison went on the Tornado

Twister three times. Guess who went on it with her?

Me! It was pretty scary, but I'm glad I tried it.

    I told you I've been busy!

Bye for now,

Megan